Sapphire Wings

A Butterfly Tale of Transformation

D1518686

Cheryl Berger

Illustrated by Stacy Jordon

WestBow Press books may be ordered through booksellers or by contacting:

WestBow Press
A Division of Thomas Nelson & Zondervan
1663 Liberty Drive
Bloomington, IN 47403
www.westbowpress.com
1 (866) 928-1240

Because of the dynamic nature of the Internet, any web addresses or links contained in this book may have changed since publication and may no longer be valid. The views expressed in this work are solely those of the author and do not necessarily reflect the views of the publisher, and the publisher hereby disclaims any responsibility for them.

Any people depicted in stock imagery provided by Thinkstock are models, and such images are being used for illustrative purposes only.
Certain stock imagery © Thinkstock.

ISBN: 978-1-9736-1416-6 (sc)
ISBN: 978-1-9736-1417-3 (e)

Library of Congress Control Number: 2017918951

Print information available on the last page.

WestBow Press rev. date: 1/27/2018

WESTBOW
P R E S S®
A DIVISION OF THOMAS NELSON
& ZONDERVAN

For my bestie, Shannon LeRoy,
who inspired me to pen this butterfly tale.
And for Jesus, who gave it wings to fly.

Caroline,

Always remember.
God sees you. God hears you.
God loves you. You are Her
sweet Caroline.

Cheryl Berger

Now this is a tale
Of transformation
Of how a larvae named Ari
Had a life renovation.

It begins in a forest
In a land far away
Where time stands still
And night shines like day.

In this far away place
Draw Near was its name
Where those seeking refuge
And miracles came.

RENOVATIONS AHEAD

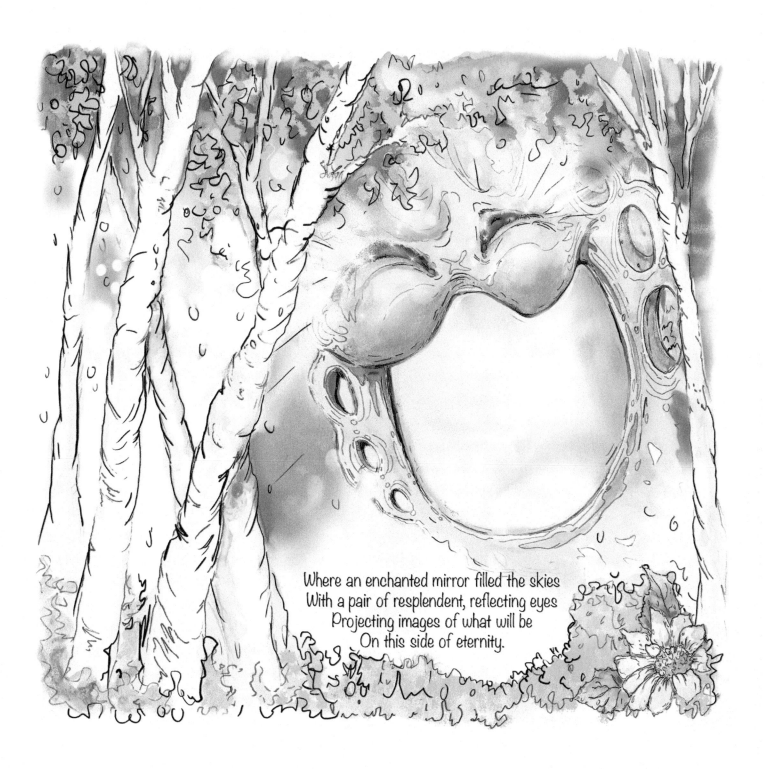

Where an enchanted mirror filled the skies
With a pair of resplendent, reflecting eyes
Projecting images of what will be
On this side of eternity.

From crimson to fuchsia
And cobalt blue,
Tangerine, yellow
And emerald green, too.

A rainbow of colors
For all to see
Surrounded a grove
Of tall mystical trees.

Where butterflies fluttered
Splendiferously
Caterpillars sojourned
Cocooned, were set free.

And the eyes of the mirror
Never slept nor turned away
No matter where one wandered
They reflected every gaze.

Now you may ask, "Come now, how can that be?
How can they always be watching over me?
And how can it be when they look at you
The eyes see countless others, too?"

Well, I'll tell you...
I don't know
But this is how
The story goes.

A larvae, named Ari, had inched from afar
To a garden of numinous trees
Her accordion-like belly rolled into a ball
On a branch made of crystal leaves.

Weary from climbing she reclined
Looking up towards the endless sky
She had but one thing on her mind
A desire, a longing to fly.

To soar over trees like the eagles
Ride the skies on a natural high
Where tiny pairs of feet morphed into wings
Under a pair of attentive eyes.

Now her journey began quite simply
On a rather ordinary day
When a voice called out from the mirror
And with affection did ask her and say.

"Butterfly, Butterfly
What do you see?
What do you see
When you look to me?

For when I look down
Here's what I see
A rainbow of colors
Flying towards Me."

"Mirror, Mirror," she replied
"How I wish your words were true
For a butterfly I do not see
When I turn my gaze towards you.

Black and white and shades of grey
With a smidge of color in between
And even more importantly
I have no flying wings."

But just as if it had not heard
The mirror said again
Words of hope to cling to
If she could only comprehend.

"Butterfly, Butterfly
To be all you were meant to be
A caterpillar renovation
Is what you will really need.

But you must not resist the process
Or trust in what your eyes can see
No, you must lay down your heart, your will, your life
And rest in Me."

Just then, a kaleidoscope of butterflies fluttered by
And Ari was sorely distracted
And instead of responding to the mirror's plea
She instinctively reacted.

Ascending to the highest limb
She leaped and closed her eyes
Intending to mount upward
Fell like a sparrow from the sky.

Still the mirror's eyes were locked on her
And did not turn away
Holding steady the eyes of the fallen one
With a concentrated gaze.

And so inching along the thorns and weeds
Onto grass made moist with dew
The caterpillar purposed now
To do what she must do.

Brushing away the prickly twigs
She crawled atop the highest tree
Spinning for herself a silken robe
Cocooned in obscurity.

Afraid it would be for nothing
That transformation would not take place
Looking one last time towards the mirror
"I trust you" became her grace.

Now it seemed for a time nothing was happening
As if she was destined to be
Bound beneath the mirrored skies
Where butterflies are free.

But suddenly there was a stirring
A tearing away of all her binding
And a vibrant rainbow of colors
Began methodically unwinding.

Shaking her head in disbelief
In awe of what her eyes did see
She flew out into the atmosphere
And soared beyond the trees.

Higher than towering mountains
She reveled in her new skin
Flapping her wings contentedly
Wonderfully born again.

"Butterfly, Butterfly," the mirror exclaimed
"Now what do you see?
Now what do you see
When you turn your eyes to Me?"

"Mirror, Mirror, she replied
"This is what I see
A miracle I did not know
Was deep inside of me.

Swirling hues like precious gems
Inlaid on sapphire wings
And a confidence in knowing
With You I can do anything.

"All I asked was to have wings to fly
But you have given so much more
A future, hope and purpose
I don't just fly; I also soar."

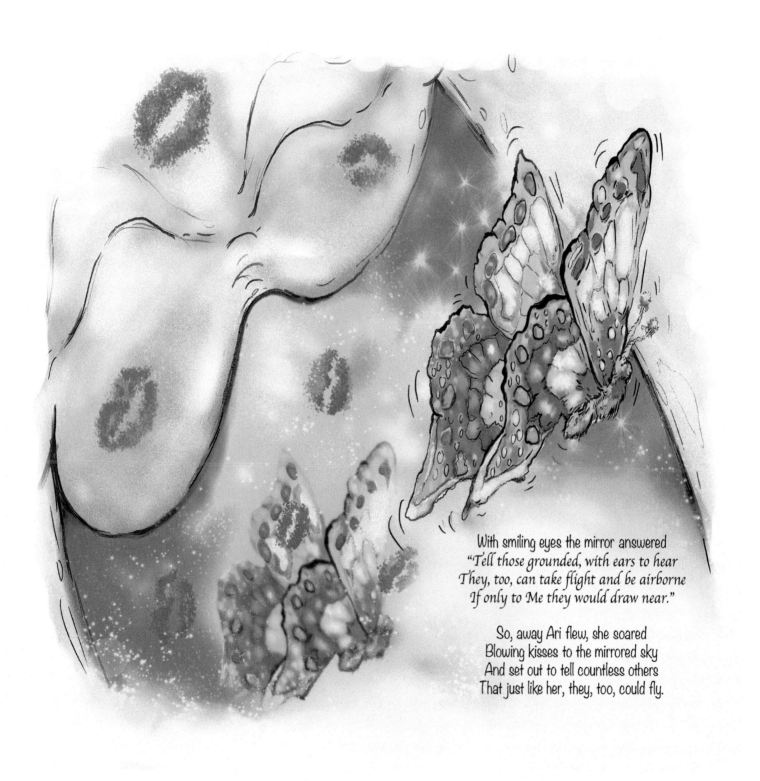

With smiling eyes the mirror answered
"Tell those grounded, with ears to hear
They, too, can take flight and be airborne
If only to Me they would draw near."

So, away Ari flew, she soared
Blowing kisses to the mirrored sky
And set out to tell countless others
That just like her, they, too, could fly.

So what now is the moral of this story
Of this butterfly fairy tale
Of a larvae who surrendered, laid down her all
Should we not do the same as well?

For like Ari in our own strength we struggle
To make the impossible come true
Forgetting it is not in our power
Only Jesus makes all things new.

We must put to rest what lies behind
Looking forward to what yet will be
So our lives will reflect His will for us
This side of eternity.

Like diamonds our eyes can shine with His light
Our ruby hearts can carry His love
Rising on sapphire wings of His presence
Drawing near to the Father above.

Listen now to Heaven's Mirror:
"My Beloved, what do you see
What do you see when you turn your eyes
Your heart, your will, towards Me?

For I have a freeway for your wilderness
For your desert I have living streams
Behold, I am doing a new thing
If you will put your trust in Me.

And so I ask again, My Beloved
Tell me what do you see
What do you see, My Beloved
What do you see when you look to Me?

What do you see, My Beloved
What do you see when you look to Me?"

And this concludes now
The tale of transformation
Of how a larvae, named Ari
Had a life renovation.

I hope you enjoyed this little rhyme
And until we meet again
With your eyes keep looking to the skies
That's it; this is ...

The End

Author Cheryl Berger ...

grew up as an Air Force military brat and has a passion for writing, the arts and loves Jesus more than chocolate. It is her hope this butterfly tale will inspire readers to see themselves through Heaven's eyes. Sapphire Wings is her second collaboration with the artist; the first being the author's devotional, Tidings of Comfort and Joy. Cheryl and her husband, Alton, have three adult children, one adorable granddaughter and two very persnickety Chihuahuas. They reside in Atlanta.

Artist Stacy Jordon ...

grew up on the outskirts of Atlanta . . . and is a true Georgia Peach. Her God, Family and Art are what make her totally complete. She has been an Artist since receiving her first crayon as a toddler and happy to say a Professional Artist for over 30 years. Married to the love of her life for 29+ years, she and Billy have two grown sons, Josh and Ethan, one horribly bratty cat, Archie and one extremely hard-headed dog, Dom. Stacy is now branching out to the world with her new on-line gallery/store
www.ArtbyStacyJ.com.

CPSIA information can be obtained
at www.ICGtesting.com
Printed in the USA
LVOW05s0051010318

568266LV00007B/18/P

9 781973 614166